Mmm, Cookies!

by Robert Munsch

Illustrated by
Michael Martchenko

Cartwheel
·B·O·O·K·S· ®

SCHOLASTIC INC.
New York Toronto London Auckland Sydney
Mexico City New Delhi Hong Kong Buenos Aires

For Chris Duggan,
Guelph, Ontario.

—R.M.

The illustrations in this book were painted in watercolor on Arches paper.

This book was designed in QuarkXPress,
with type set in 20 point Caslon 244 Medium.

ISBN 0-590-89604-0

Library of Congress Cataloging-in-Publication Data available

15 14 13 12   07 08 09

Printed in the U.S.A.   23
This edition first printing, April 2002

Mom's Play Clay Recipe

Heat to boiling:

1 1/2 cups water

1/2 cup salt

Add:

2 tsp. food coloring

2 tbsp. alum

2 tbsp. salad oil

2 cups (or more) flour

Knead well.

Store in plastic wrap.

Make sure an adult does the heating! Never use a stove without an adult to help you.

Christopher walked down into the basement and saw a big pile of play clay in the corner.

"Wow!" said Christopher. "I love play clay."

So he got himself a piece of red
play clay and whapped it in his hands —
WHAP, WHAP, WHAP, WHAP, WHAP.
Made it nice and round —
SWISH, SWISH, SWISH, SWISH, SWISH.
Sprinkled it with sugar —
CHIK, CHIK, CHIK, CHIK, CHIK.
Covered it with yellow icing —
Glick, Glick, Glick, Glick, Glick.
And put some raisins on top —
PLUNK, PLUNK, PLUNK, PLUNK, PLUNK.

Then Christopher went upstairs and said, "Mommy, look! Daddy made you a cookie!"

"Ohhhhh!" said his mother. "That's so nice! I didn't even know he could cook."

So she picked up that cookie
and took a big bite.

SCRRUUUNNNNCH!

And she yelled, "YUCK!
PWAH! SPLICHT!
PLAY CLAY!
GLA-GLA-GLA-GLA!"

8

She ran to the bathroom and washed
out her mouth for a long time —

SCRITCH-SCRITCH,
SCRITCH-SCRITCH,
SCRITCH-SCRITCH.

While his mother was washing out her
mouth, Christopher got himself another
piece of red play clay.

He whapped it in his hands —
WHAP, WHAP, WHAP, WHAP, WHAP.
Made it nice and round —
SWISH, SWISH, SWISH, SWISH, SWISH.
Sprinkled it with sugar —
CHIK, CHIK, CHIK, CHIK, CHIK.
Covered it with yellow icing —
Glick, Glick, Glick, Glick, Glick.
And put some raisins on top —
PLUNK, PLUNK, PLUNK, PLUNK, PLUNK.
Then he went upstairs to find his father.

Christopher said, "Daddy, look! Mommy made you a cookie."

"Ohhhhh!" said his father. "That's so nice! It's been a long time since your mother made me cookies."

So he picked it up and took a big bite.

SCRRUUUNNNNCH!

And he yelled, "YUCK!
PWAH! SPLICHT!
PLAY CLAY!
GLA-GLA-GLA-GLA!"

That cookie tasted so bad, he ran
to the bathroom and washed out
his mouth.

SCRITCH-SCRITCH,
SCRITCH-SCRITCH,
SCRITCH-SCRITCH.

By the time his father and mother came out of the bathroom, Christopher was late for school.

So they called up the teacher and said, "Christopher is giving people PLAY CLAY cookies!"

"Don't worry," said the teacher. "I know just what to do."

She got herself some red play clay and
whapped it in her hands —
WHAP, WHAP, WHAP, WHAP, WHAP.
Made it nice and round —
SWISH, SWISH, SWISH, SWISH, SWISH.
Sprinkled it with sugar —
CHIK, CHIK, CHIK, CHIK, CHIK.
Covered it with yellow icing —
Glick, Glick, Glick, Glick, Glick.
And put some raisins on top —
PLUNK, PLUNK, PLUNK, PLUNK, PLUNK.
Then she put the cookie on
Christopher's chair.

When Christopher came in, he
said, "Look at the lovely cookie!"
He picked it up and took a big bite.

SCRRUUUNNNNCH!

And he yelled, "YUCK!
PWAH! SPLICHT!
PLAY CLAY!
GLA-GLA-GLA-GLA!"

That cookie tasted so bad, he ran
to the bathroom and washed out
his mouth.

BURBLE

BURBLE SPLAT

SPLICHT

BWAHHH.

24

When Christopher came back from the bathroom, the teacher said, "And now would everyone like to make some REAL cookies?"
And the class yelled "YES!"

And when Christopher was done
with his cookie . . .

he took it home to give to his
mother and father.